DO-WAH ROCKS!

SCHOLASTIC INC.

New York Toronto London Auckland Sydney
Mexico City New Delhi Hong Kong Buenos Aires

Written by Gerry Bailey

ISBN 0-439-37561-4

Illustrations by Henryk Szor of Advocate
Visualizations by Catherine MacKinnon

Produced by Scholastic Inc. in 2001 under license from Just Licensing Ltd.

12 11 10 9 8 7 6 5 4 3 2 1 2 3 4 5 6 7/0

Printed in the U.S.A.
First Scholastic printing, January 2002

It is the year 2053. The Butt-Ugly Martians have been sent by their leader, the evil Emperor Bog, and his nightmarish henchman, Dr. Damage, to invade Earth! Their own planet, Mars, was destroyed in a minor incident, which the Martians refer to as "Oops," and they need a new home.

But instead of conquering the planet, the three fun-loving Martians fall for the place and befriend three kids, Mike, Angela, and Cedric. Together, they spend their time protecting the planet, both from Emperor Bog and any other alien that might try to destroy it.

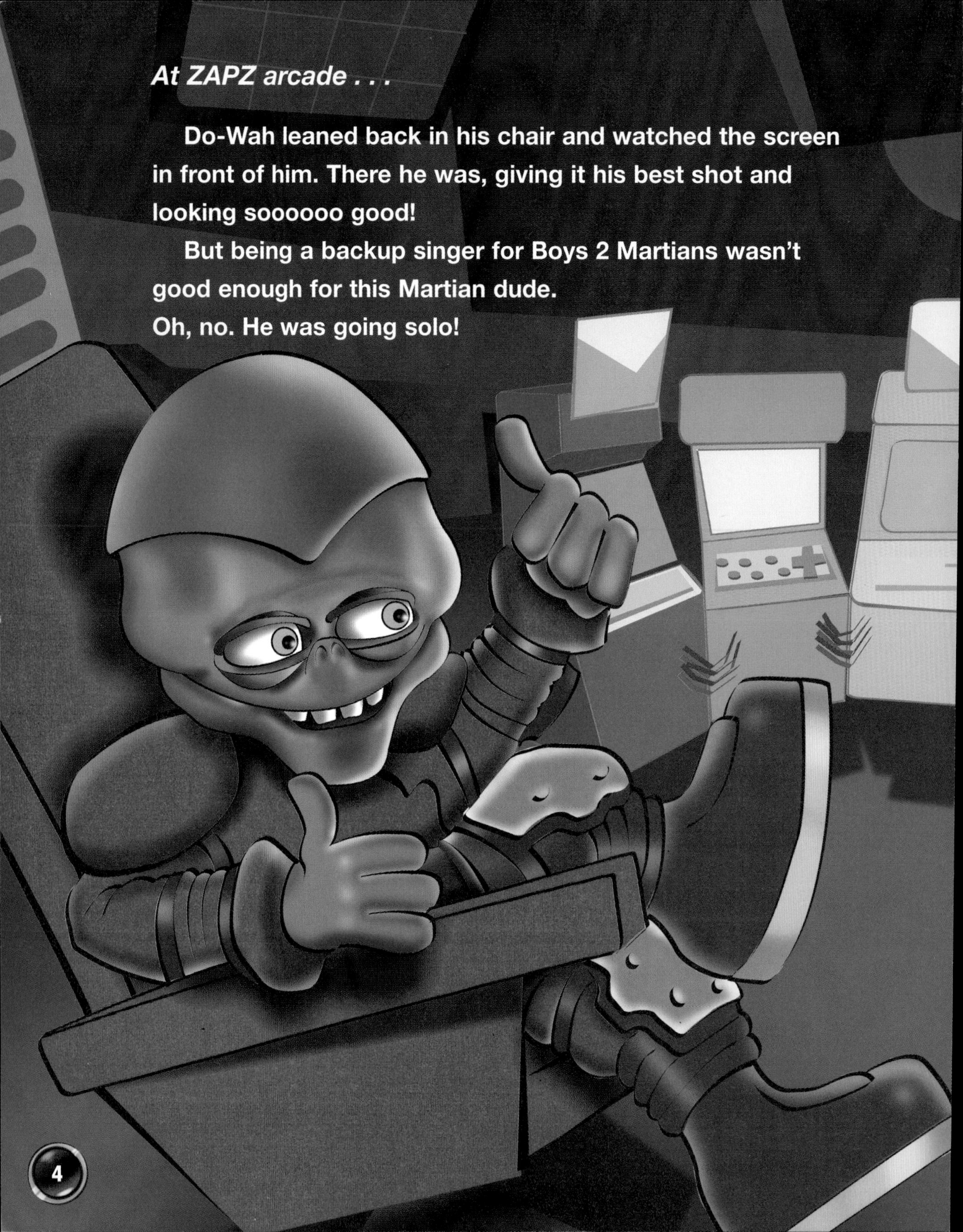

At ZAPZ arcade . . .

Do-Wah leaned back in his chair and watched the screen in front of him. There he was, giving it his best shot and looking soooooo good!

But being a backup singer for Boys 2 Martians wasn't good enough for this Martian dude.

Oh, no. He was going solo!

"Hey, Martian," said Do-Wah, grinning at the screen. "You sound so good you're even better than me. Wait a minute — you are me! Wow, if I'm groovin' this good, I've got to get a career in music. I'll send a demo to Syd Severe right now."

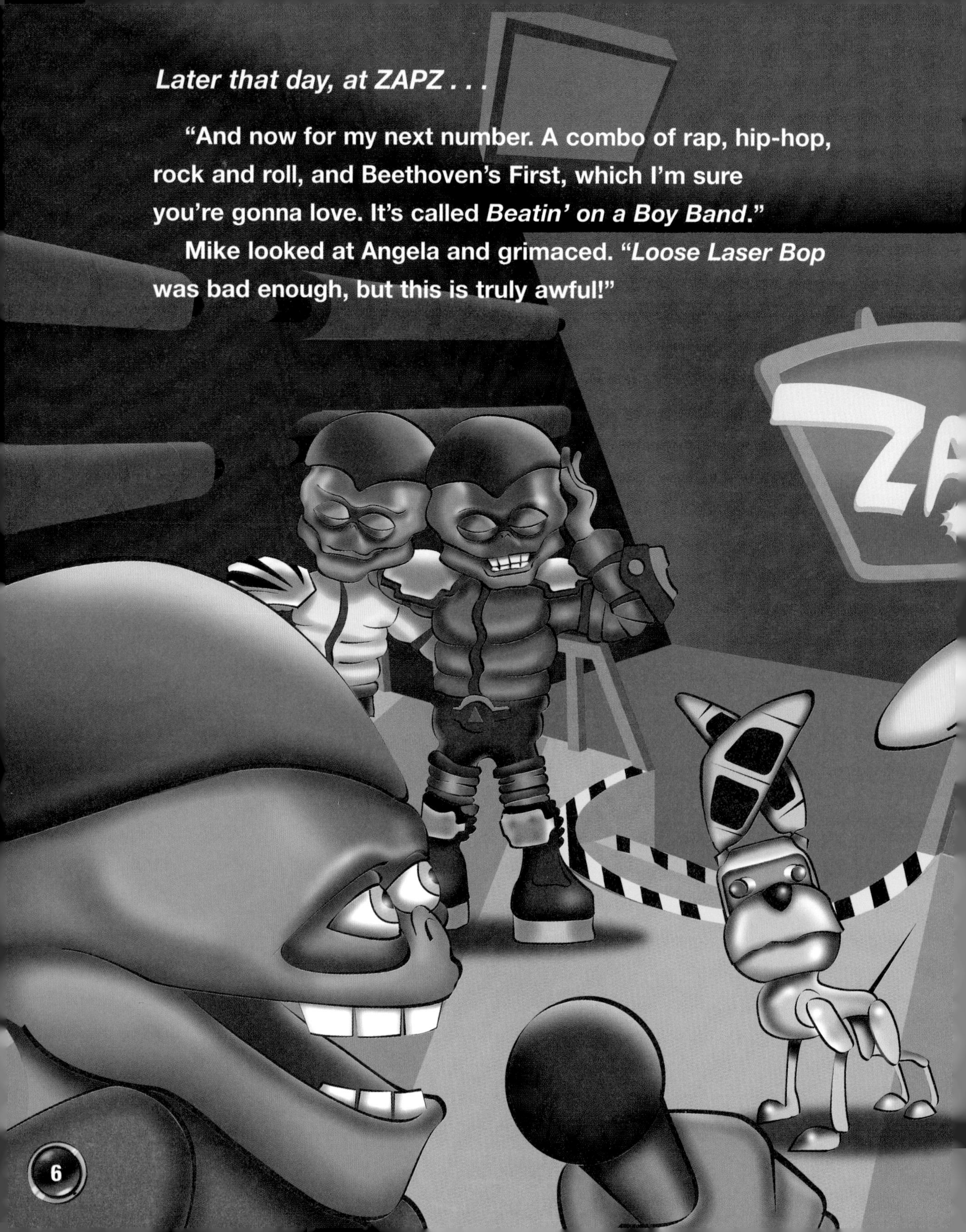

Later that day, at ZAPZ . . .

"And now for my next number. A combo of rap, hip-hop, rock and roll, and Beethoven's First, which I'm sure you're gonna love. It's called *Beatin' on a Boy Band*."

Mike looked at Angela and grimaced. "*Loose Laser Bop* was bad enough, but this is truly awful!"

"Ex-cru-ti-ating," said Cedric, covering his ears.

Do-Wah finished the song, put down the mike, and grinned at his audience. "I'm gonna be massive!"

"Yeah!" cried B.Bop. "Then when some hideous alien comes along, we can just get you to sing to it."

On the Bogstar *. . .*

As Do-Wah waited for Syd Severe's eloquent critique of his musical talents, the equally talented Dr. Damage was at work in his laboratory aboard the *Bogstar*.

"That should do it," he said, looking at the Rekonobot spy robot, Klaktor. "Now get down to Earth and crunch a few Earthlings. And don't forget those ridiculous Martians that Bog calls 'advance troops.' The only advance they'll make is into an early grave, ha — haaaaaaah!"

Damage watched as Klaktor made his way out of the lab. "BYEEEE," he dribbled.

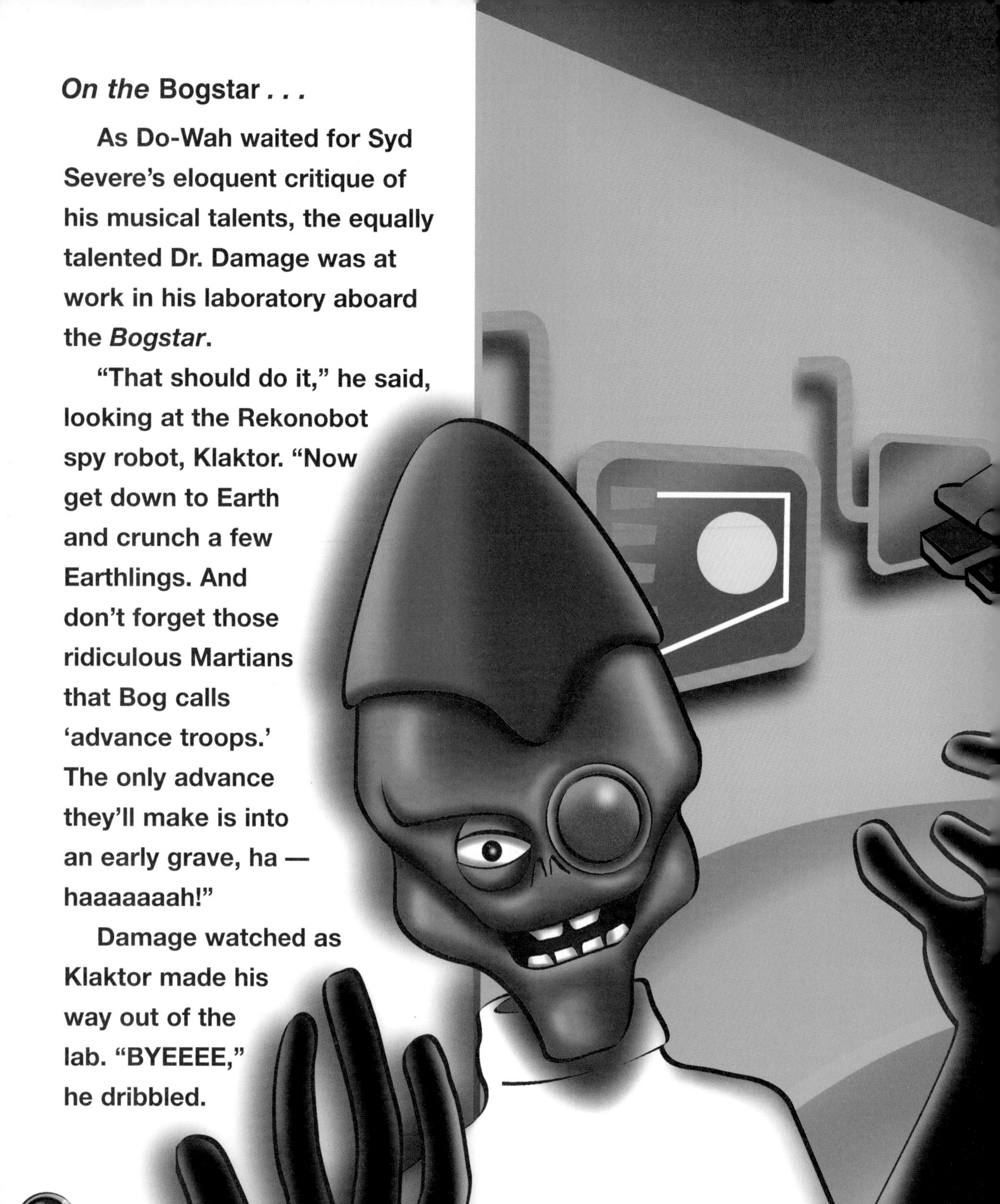

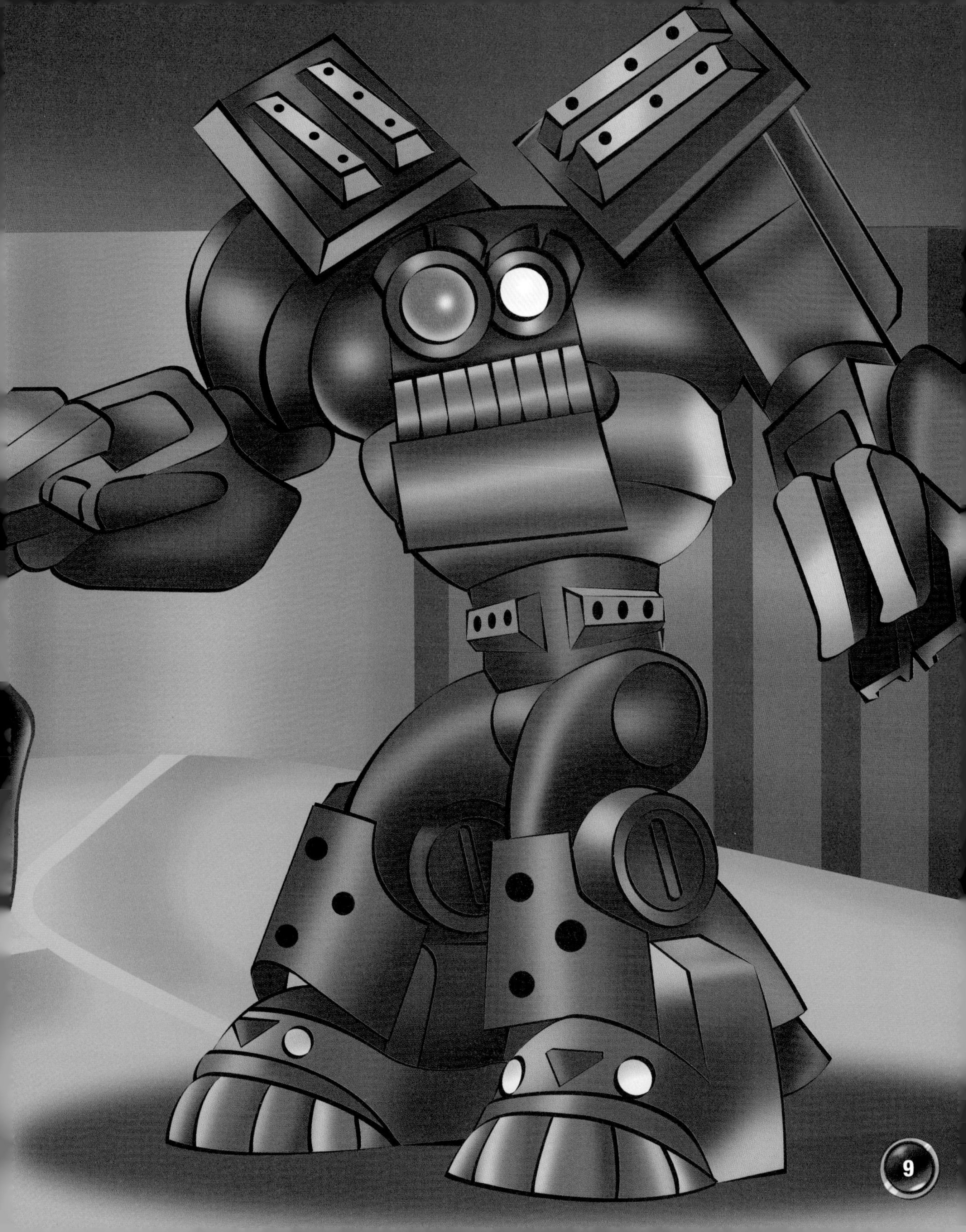

Back at ZAPZ arcade . . .

"Hey, Dog — I've made it!" cried Do-Wah to Dog. "I've been accepted by Syd Severe. Now all I have to do is perfect my dance routine. Come on Dog, you can be my dance buddy, and we'll go at it just like they do on the *Slop of the Pops* show."

Do-Wah showed Dog the moves and turned on the music. Together, they jived across the floor in perfect sync.

At Mike's house . . .

Mike switched on the television as the others settled down to watch Syd Severe's weekly music show, *Slop of the Pops*.

"Here are our coolest dudes, the very baddest, Do-Wah and Dog," Syd said.

"What did he say?" yelled B.Bop as bits of his pizza did a midair flip.

"They'll find out he's an alien, for sure," said Cedric.

"You know, he's not that bad." B.Bop smiled.

"Perhaps . . ."

"Don't even think about it!" yelled Mike. "Come on. We've got to get him out of there!"

The kids hopped on their hoverboards, while B.Bop and 2-T zoomed into view aboard their OMABs.

"Let's go!" shouted Mike. "Follow me and try not to look too conspicuous."

"Con what?" said 2-T.

"Try not to be seen," explained Angela. In a cloud of dust, the rescuers headed downtown.

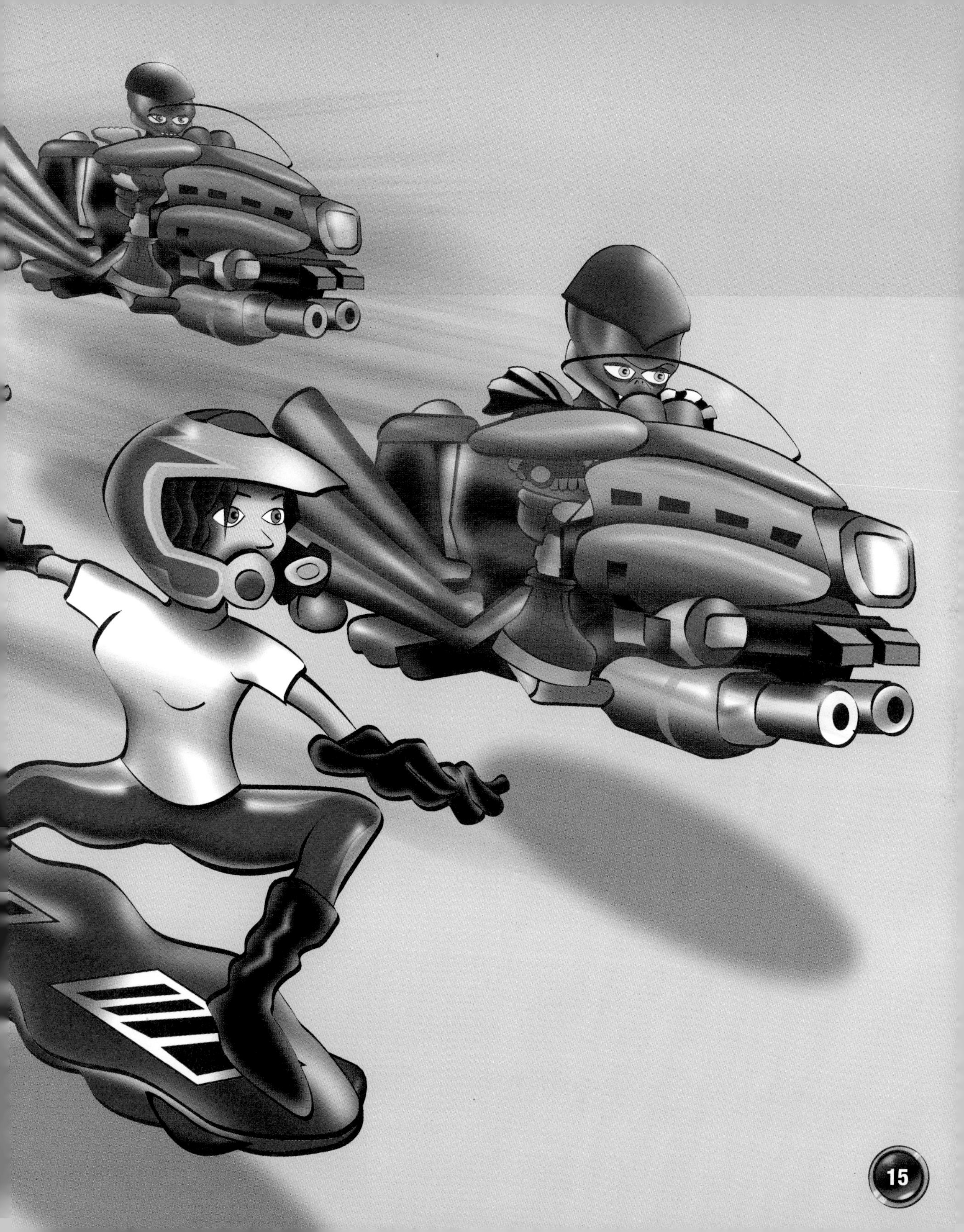

At Quantum Burgers . . .

Ronald, the counter nerd at Quantum Burgers, was watching the show too. He looked puzzled.

"That music . . ." he said as he slowly and lovingly wiped a ketchup-splattered counter, "it's terrible — it's not even human! . . ." He grimaced. And then, it hit him. "That's it!" he yelled. "That's no superstar in the making. That's an alien!"

Ronald rushed to his secret transponder and switched onto the wavelength of his hero, Stoat Muldoon: Alien Hunter.

Inside Stoat Muldoon's missile silo headquarters . . .

"What's that?" said Muldoon. "You don't mean . . ."

Muldoon turned on his video screen. A look of horror mixed with glee contorted his chiseled features. "This is it. I'm going to capture that alien. No one sings like that in front of Stoat Muldoon and gets away with it."

Muldoon quickly boarded his hovervan and headed for the TV station.

Somewhere in the desert . . .

Not far away, hidden in the desert sands, Klaktor lurked. He had intercepted the conversation between Ronald and Muldoon, and reported it back to Damage.

"I have located some Earthlings — and those ridiculous Martians of whom you speak. I shall exterminate them."

"Well done," answered Damage. "Keep me informed."

Outside the TV station . . .

"Here we are," said Mike. "Oh, no, there's a guard on the door — and he's real big!"

"You can't come in here," said the guard. "Only stars and hangers-on are allowed in here."

"Hmmm. Hanger-on," said B.Bop, smiling. Then he shot a solid light rope from his wrist gauntlet, wound it round the guard, tied him up, and hung him from a sign just beside the door.

Mike led the kids, B.Bop, and 2-T through the entrance and down to the live studio in the basement. They arrived just as the curtain was coming down on Do-Wah's act.

Inside the TV station . . .

"More, more!" shouted the audience.

"Are they all deaf?" asked B.Bop.

"By now they are, babe," said 2-T.

"Cut the gab and get him out of there," said Mike anxiously.

B.Bop grabbed Do-Wah and Dog, and the gang headed offstage. But as they reached a sign saying UP, they stopped in their tracks.

Ahead of them, barring the way, was none other than Stoat Muldoon: Alien Hunter!

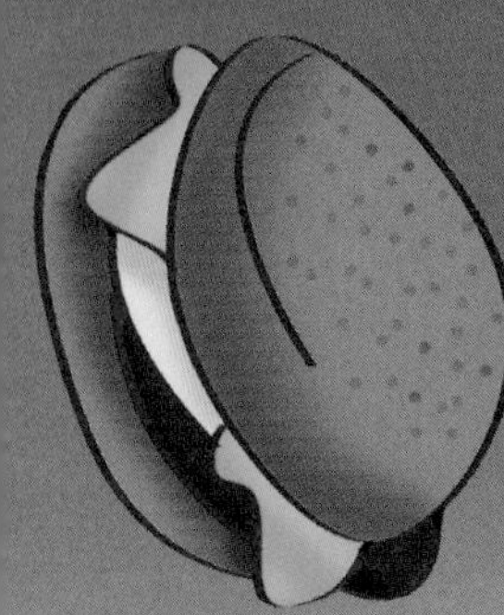

They turned and ran as fast as they could. Muldoon followed, but as he crossed the stage, he saw the audience and stopped.

What an opportunity, he thought. *Fate has brought me here. I must obey*.

And with that, Muldoon broke into his favorite song, *She'll Be Coming Round the Mountain.* It didn't go well!

"Get that dopey dude off."

"The guy's in a time warp."

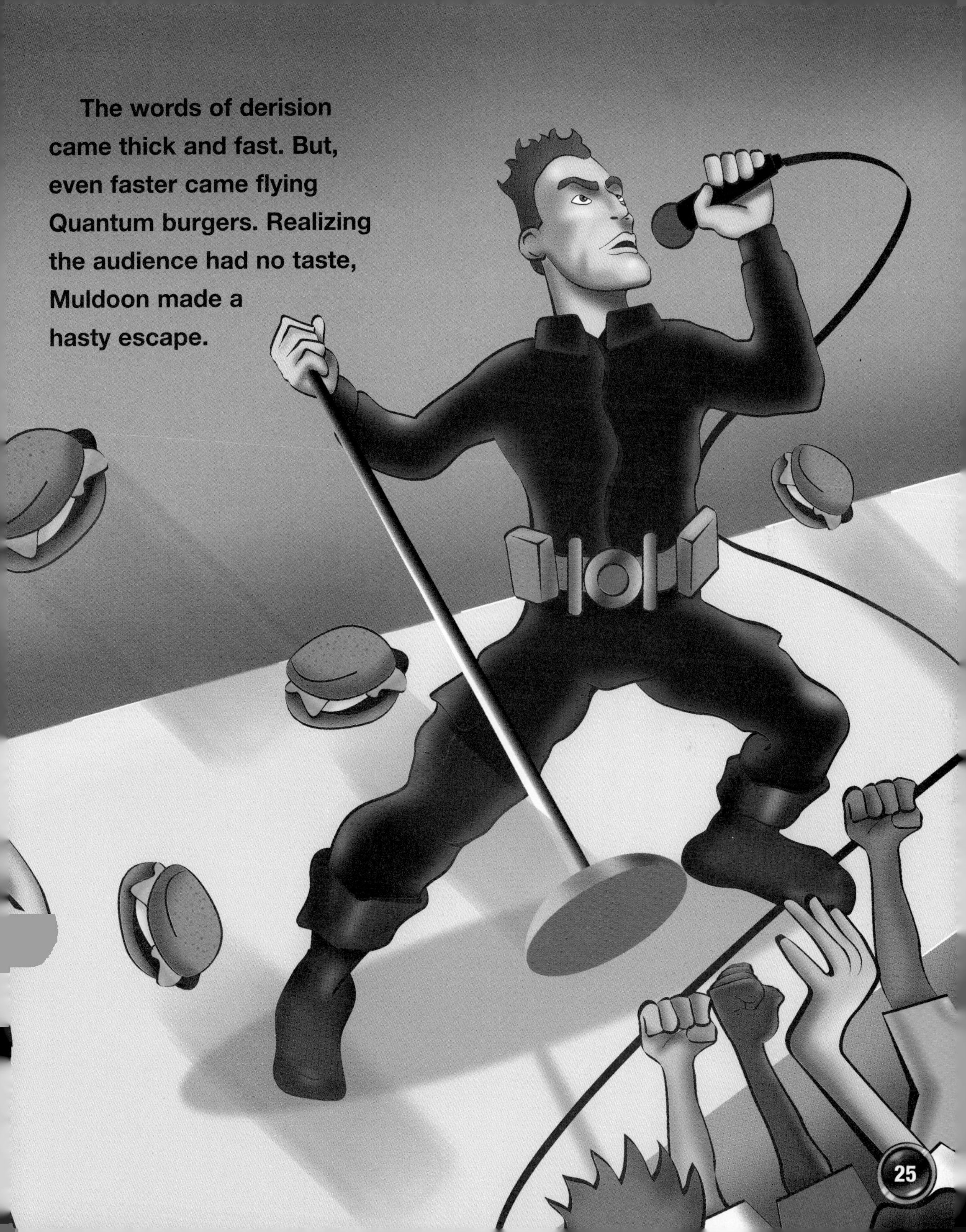

The words of derision came thick and fast. But, even faster came flying Quantum burgers. Realizing the audience had no taste, Muldoon made a hasty escape.

On the roof of the TV station . . .

Meanwhile, the gang had found its way onto the roof of the building. There was nowhere else to run to — there was no way forward and no way back!

"Looks like Muldoon's got us now," said Mike. But just then he caught sight of Klaktor. "What in hamburger heaven is that?"

The spy robot was looming in front of them all.

Wasting no time, B.Bop yelled, "LET'S GET UGLY!" And the three Martians slammed into B.K.M.

Let's Get Ugly!

"Double plus one," ordered B.Bop.

Do-Wah streaked into the sky above Klaktor's head, while the other two Martians raced toward him. They leaped into the air and each grabbed an arm.

Klaktor flexed his arms and, with a massive surge of energy, threw off B.Bop and 2-T.

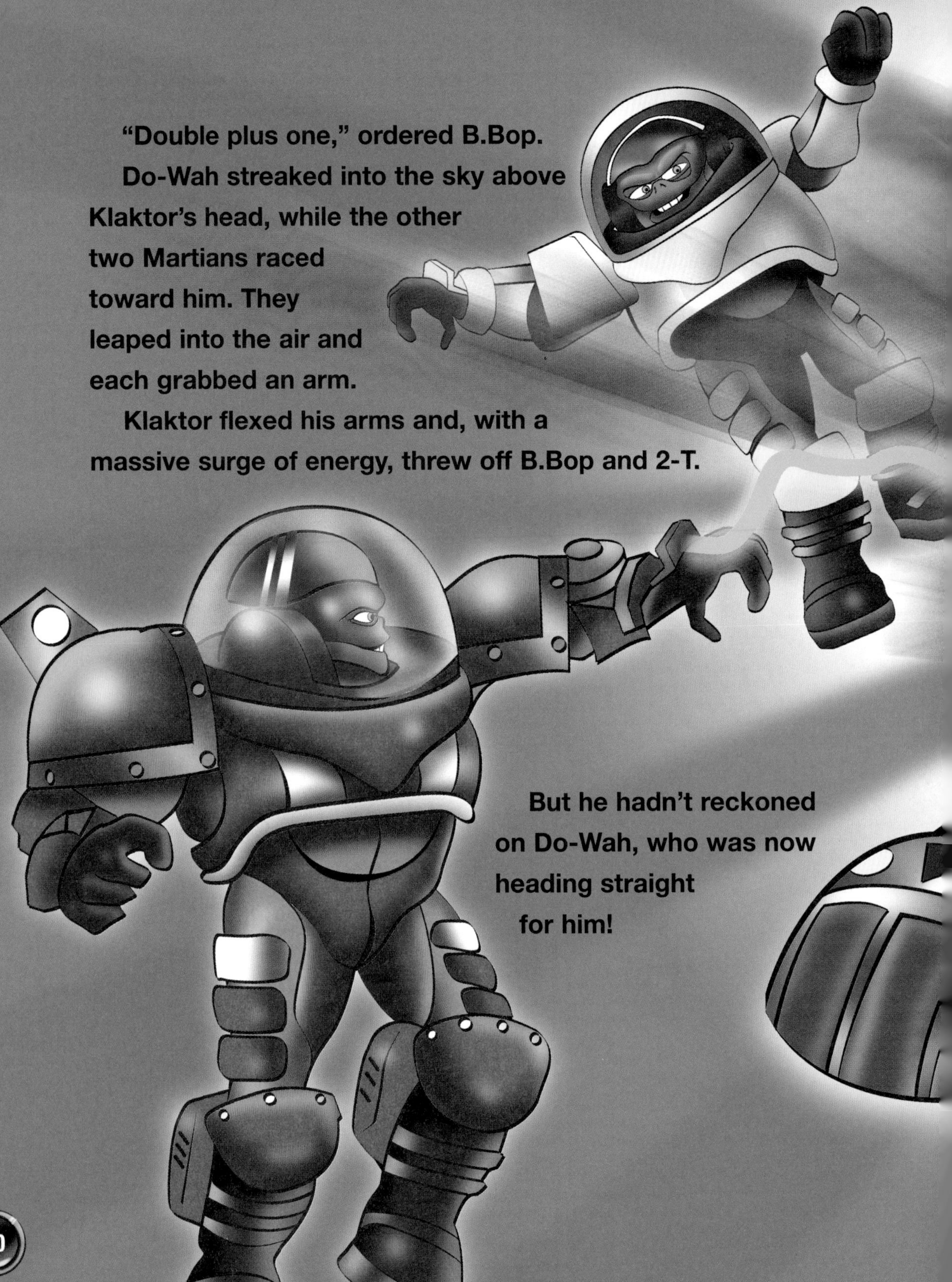

But he hadn't reckoned on Do-Wah, who was now heading straight for him!

"Nice knowing you!" Do-Wah yelled as he speared Klaktor with an energy bolt. The robot was totally destroyed, as bits of it flew in all directions.

The Martians then swept down and each grabbed one of their Earthling friends. Muldoon was speechless when he arrived to find everyone had vanished.

"Wow!" cried Mike. "A free flight home."

"Just in time to hear my new single." Do-Wah laughed.

"Please, no more singing," groaned Mike.

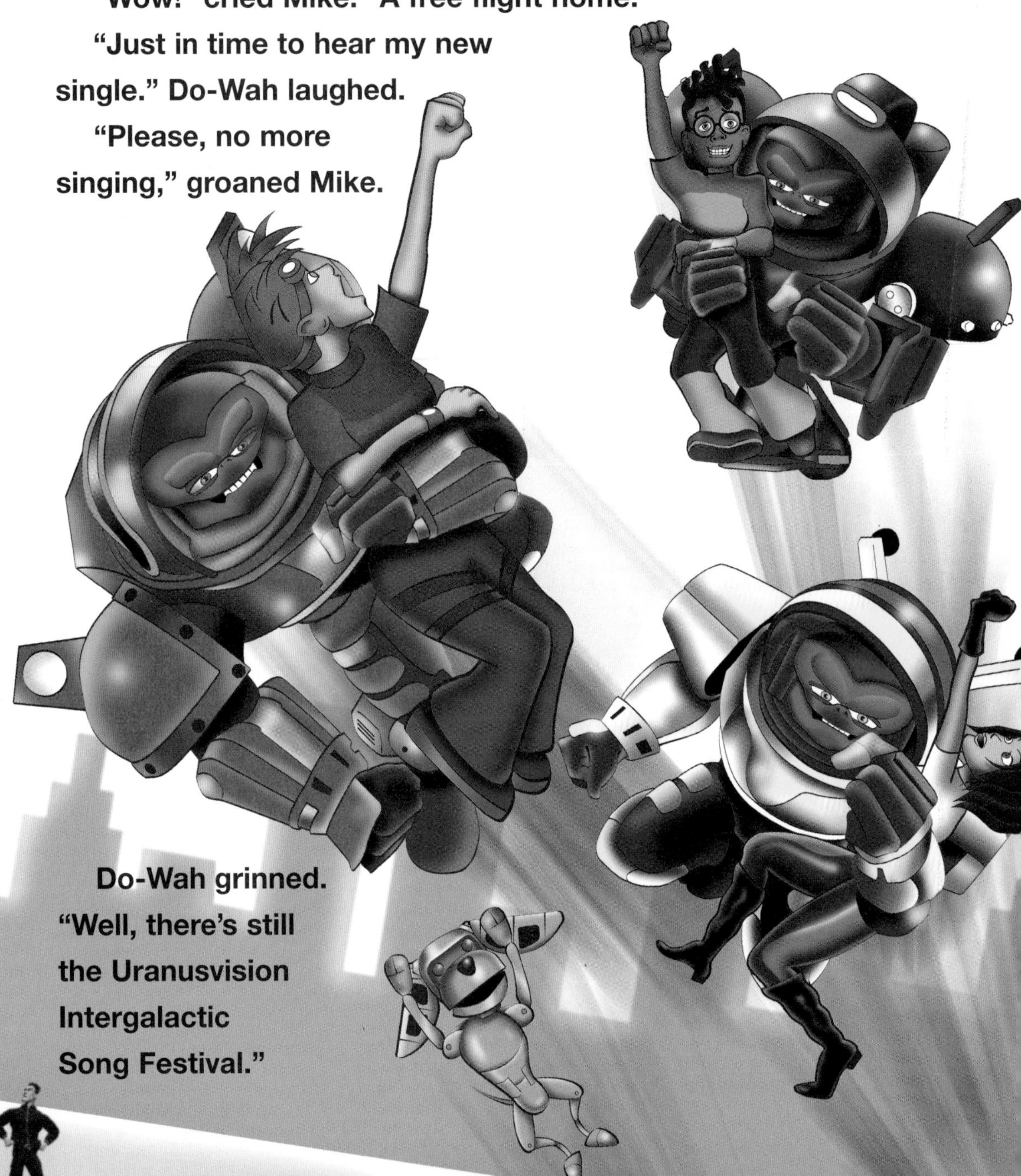

Do-Wah grinned. "Well, there's still the Uranusvision Intergalactic Song Festival."